STORMS!

Written by Rick Leslie

STECK-VAUGHN
C O M P A N Y
ELEMENTARY • SECONDARY • ADULT • LIBRARY

THUNDERSTORM

TORNADO

HURRICANE

HAIL STORM

BLIZZARD

ICE STORM

The sky fills with clouds. The sun disappears. Heavy rains begin. Strong winds blow. Windows rattle. Everyone runs inside. A storm is coming!

THUNDERSTORMS

Thunderstorms have lightning and thunder. Lightning is the bright flash in a thunderstorm. The flash is an electric charge that heats up the air. The hot air makes a booming sound called thunder. Heavy rain often comes with a thunderstorm.

TORNADOES

Tornadoes are powerful storms. They have very strong winds. These winds blow around and around in a circle. They form a cloud shaped like a cone. Sometimes the cloud drops down and moves along the ground. Then it damages nearly everything in its path. Tornadoes are sometimes called twisters.

HURRICANES

Hurricanes are dangerous wind storms. Winds in a hurricane blow over 70 miles per hour. That is as fast as a speeding car going down a highway. Hurricanes usually stay over the ocean. When they move onto land, they cause great damage.

9

HAIL STORMS

In some storms, rain and snow mix together to form hail. These chunks of ice are very hard. They can be as large as baseballs. Hail storms usually begin suddenly and last only a short time. Still, they can cause a lot of damage.

BLIZZARDS

Blizzards are terrible snow storms. They bring heavy winds and freezing temperatures. Often you cannot see during a blizzard. The snow and wind seem to form a giant white sheet. A blizzard blankets the ground with lots of snow. Sometimes it can take days to dig out of a blizzard.

ICE STORMS

An ice storm is caused by rain that falls when it is freezing outside. This kind of storm is very dangerous. When the rain freezes, it turns into sleet. Then everything is coated with a thin sheet of ice. Icy roads and sidewalks become very slippery. This makes it hard for people to drive and walk places.

15

STORM WARNINGS

Weather watchers warn people when a storm is forming. They tell how strong the storm might be. They tell when it is coming and where it could hit. People can get ready for a storm when they are warned by a weather watcher. The more people know about storms, the safer they can be.